**LADYBIRD BOOKS**

UK | USA | Canada | Ireland | Australia | India | New Zealand | South Africa

Ladybird Books is part of the Penguin Random House group of companies
whose addresses can be found at global.penguinrandomhouse.com.

www.penguin.co.uk    www.puffin.co.uk    www.ladybird.co.uk

 Penguin
Random House
UK

First published 2022
001

© 2022 ABD Ltd/Ent. One UK Ltd/Hasbro
Adapted by Lauren Holowaty

Licensed by

Printed in China

The authorized representative in the EEA is Penguin Random House Ireland,
Morrison Chambers, 32 Nassau Street, Dublin D02 YH68

A CIP catalogue record for this book is available from the British Library

ISBN: 978-0-241-54341-2

All correspondence to:
Ladybird Books, Penguin Random House Children's
One Embassy Gardens, 8 Viaduct Gardens, London SW11 7BW

**FSC**
www.fsc.org

MIX
Paper from
responsible sources
FSC® C018179

# Peppa
## the
# Zookeeper

It was breakfast time, and Mummy and Daddy Pig had a **big** surprise for Peppa. "We're going to the zoo!" announced Daddy Pig. "You're going to be a zookeeper for the day!"

"Wow!" cried Peppa. "What do zookeepers do?"

"Excellent question, Peppa!" said Daddy Pig. "That's what we're going there to find out!"

"Hooray!" cheered Peppa.

Peppa was so excited that she sang all the way to the zoo.

"Bing-bong-bing,
Bong-bing-boo,
I am going to the zoo!"

When they arrived, Mr Lion the zookeeper was waiting at the gate.
"Hello, Peppa," he said. "I hear you are helping us today."
"Yes!" cried Peppa. "What does a zookeeper do?"
"First, you must put on your important zookeeper's clothes,"
said Mr Lion, passing a uniform to Peppa.

It was very early, and there were no visitors in the zoo yet.
"We need to get breakfast ready," said Mr Lion.
"Can you help pick some lettuce?"
"Lettuce?" said Peppa. "For breakfast?"
"Yuck!" said George.
"It's the tortoises' favourite," explained Mr Lion.

Peppa and George picked all the lettuce.
"Is this enough?" asked Peppa.

"Er . . . Plenty!" said Mr Lion,
looking at the empty lettuce patches.

Peppa helped Mr Lion feed the tortoises some lettuce. Breakfast with the tortoises was lots of fun!

Munch! Munch!

Crrrunch!

"They're very hungry, aren't they?" said Peppa.
"They are indeed," said Mr Lion.

Peppa pretended to be a tortoise, moving slowly and
munching on lettuce. "*Munch, munch, crrrunch!*"
"You look just like a tortoise, Peppa," said Daddy Pig, chuckling.
"I love looking after the tortoises," said Peppa. "But what
else does a zookeeper do?"
"I'll show you!" said Mr Lion. "We keep
everyone happy at the zoo!"

Mr Lion took everyone to check on the butterflies.
"Do butterflies eat lettuce for breakfast?" asked Peppa.
"Butterflies get their food and drink from flowers," said
Mr Giraffe, who looked after the butterflies.

Peppa watched the butterflies slurp from the flowers.
"*Flutter! Flutter! Slurp! Slurp!*" said Peppa, pretending to
be a butterfly.
George giggled. "*Sluurrppp!* Hee! Hee!"

"What else does a zookeeper do?" asked Peppa. "This is Mrs Crocodile," said Mr Lion. "She is the zookeeper in charge of the penguins."

"Hello, Mrs Crocodile," said Peppa.
"What are you doing?"
"I'm feeding the penguins some fish,"
replied Mrs Crocodile. "Would you
like to help?"
"Ooh!" cried Peppa. "Yes, please!"

Peppa and Mrs Crocodile threw fish to the penguins.
The penguins were very good at catching them.

"*Waddle! Waddle! Catch!*" said Peppa, pretending to be a penguin.
"You look just like a penguin, Peppa," said Mummy Pig.
Everyone laughed when they saw Peppa waddle . . .
even the penguins!
"That was amazing," said Peppa. "What else does a
zookeeper do?"

Hee! Hee!

Hee! Hee!

Hee! Hee!

Mr Lion rolled up on the zoo train to collect
Peppa and her family.
"*Choo! Choo!*" cried George.
"Where are we going now, Mr Lion?" asked Peppa.

"To check on the tiny creatures," said Mr Lion.
"First stop – the Wild Wood."
"How exciting," said Daddy Pig.
"Hooray!" cheered Peppa and George.

"I can't see any tiny creatures," said Peppa when they got to the wood.
Mr Lion gave Peppa a magnifying glass. It made tiny things look big.

"Look! A ladybird," said Peppa. "What does she eat?"
"Smaller insects that she finds in the wild,"
explained Mr Lion.
"So we don't need to feed her breakfast?"
asked Peppa.
"No," said Mr Lion. "There are
lots of things she can eat
right here in the wood."

After the Wild Wood, Mr Lion drove Peppa and her family all around the zoo.

"Now everyone's had breakfast, what do we do?" asked Peppa.

"Lunch!" said Mr Lion.

"It's feeding time?" said Peppa. "Again?"

"It's always feeding time at the zoo!" said Mr Lion.

"But what do we feed the tortoises?" asked Peppa. "There's no more lettuce, and it's their favourite!"
"We'll have to find something else," said Mr Lion, frowning.
Just then, Peppa had an idea . . .

"My granny and grandpa grow lettuce in their garden,"
said Peppa. "We could get some from them!"
"What a wonderful idea, Peppa," said Mummy Pig.

"That would be fantastic," said Mr Lion. "All aboard the zoo train! Next stop – Granny and Grandpa Pig's house!"
"*Choo! Choo!*" cheered George.

Peppa and her family hopped on the zoo train with Mr Lion. They trundled out of the zoo, down the road and all the way to Granny and Grandpa Pig's house.

"Hello, little ones," said Granny and Grandpa Pig as the zoo train pulled up outside their house.

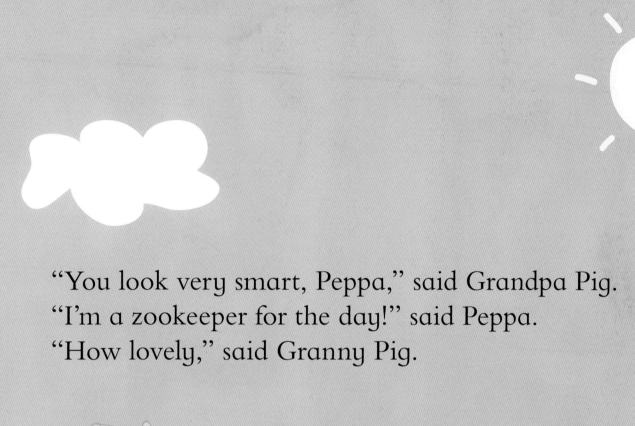

"You look very smart, Peppa," said Grandpa Pig.
"I'm a zookeeper for the day!" said Peppa.
"How lovely," said Granny Pig.

Peppa explained that the zoo needed Granny and
Grandpa Pig's help. "We've run out of lettuce," she said,
"and the tortoises want some for lunch."
"Well," said Grandpa Pig, "we can certainly help with that!"

Grandpa Pig took everyone to his vegetable patch, and they got picking. Soon, they had filled the zoo train with lettuce!

"Thank you, Granny and Grandpa," said Peppa.
"Yes, thank you very much," added Mr Lion.
"You're most welcome," said Grandpa Pig. "Happy to help!"

Back at the zoo, the tortoises were very happy with their lovely lettuce lunch. "What a **fantastic** zookeeper you are, Peppa!" said Mr Lion. "You've looked after the animals and made them feel safe and happy!"

Munch!

Munch!

"Being a zookeeper is fun," said Peppa. "Who do we need to feed next?"
"US!" said Mr Lion. "It's feeding time for the zookeepers! Let's wash our hands and have our own lunch."

Crunch!

Peppa and her family sat with the other zookeepers.
"Fancy some lettuce for lunch, Peppa?" asked Daddy Pig.
"Yes please, Daddy!" said Peppa. "I love being a zookeeper . . .
because it's always feeding time at the zoo!"

Peppa loves being a zookeeper.
Everyone loves being a zookeeper!